D0885045

Verse in Arabic is ... *the kind of book that stays with you long after you've turned the last page.*

— BILL THOMPSON
Radio journalist and host of *The Bookcast*

I don't like mysteries. I lose interest quickly and if I persevere to the end, I am almost always disappointed. Birgitte Rasine has taught me a lesson with her artfully and hypnotically composed **Verse in Arabic**. *Based on a real life story that haunted her for decades, this is a book that defies many of the conventional "rules" of fiction writing.*

Rasine is a master wordsmith, whose prose is graceful and poetic, yet efficient and, for that reason, effective. Every word counts, and you'll hang on every word as well.

I may have to rethink my aversion to mysteries—especially if they're written by Birgitte Rasine.

— CYNTHIA DAGNAL-MYRON
Author and award-winning former journalist for the *Chicago Sun Times*

No ending will suffice for a mystery that will remain in the reader's mind as a companion long after the last page. The author wants you as an accomplice, and succeeds masterfully. Madrid, medicine, innocence and crime, tall verse written for your pleasure by this brilliant author. Shokran!

— ISABEL CAMPOY
Author and former Senior Editor at Houghton Mifflin Harcourt

*Birgitte Rasine's mysterious **Verse in Arabic** pulled me in and held me from beginning to end. Beautifully written, this story continues to demonstrate that Rasine is an uncommonly gifted writer.*

— DON THOMPSON
Author, playwright, and film producer

***Verse in Arabic** is a captivating tale of murder, innocence, and intrigue. It is set in Spain during a complex and turbulent period in that country's history. The writing is crisp and visual; the characters are compelling and developed caringly and with precision. The author's careful unraveling of information and details—a methodical crescendo, sentence by sentence, paragraph by paragraph—is masterful storytelling.*

*Once you start reading, you will find it a challenge to put **Verse in Arabic** down.*

— STEVE KAFFEN
Author and member of The Explorers Club

Verse in Arabic

Other works by Birgitte Rasine

Books
The Serpent and the Jaguar: Living in Sacred Time

Short Stories
The Visionary
(upcoming)

Confession

Bakaly

The Seventh Crane

Mobile Apps
(author and producer)
MCP Mayan Tzolkin

My Mayan Match

Verse in Arabic

BIRGITTE RASINE

A

SURFACETENSION

B O O K

LUCITÀ
PUBLISHING

Published in the United States by
LUCITÀ Publishing, an imprint of LUCITÀ Inc.
P.O. Box 70746
Sunnyvale, CA 94086-0746
http://publishing.lucita.net

ISBN-13: 978-19382840-2-1

Library of Congress Control Number: 2012906394

This is a "Surface Tension" book.
First LUCITÀ Publishing edition 2013.
LUCITÀ and the sun logo are trademarks of LUCITÀ, Inc.

Cover and book design by LUCITÀ Inc.

Visit *www.birgitterasine.com* for more information about Birgitte Rasine and her work.

Printed in the United States of America on FSC-certified, 30% post consumer recycled paper.

to Bernardo

CONTENTS

Verse in Arabic

I didn't notice the rays of the rising sun slipping through the wet branches of the tall nameless trees we passed by; I didn't see the emptiness of the streets we drove through; I cared nothing for the worries all those people flitting past my rain-strewn window carried deep inside. I didn't feel the cobblestones rumbling beneath the wheels: all I could think about was *him*.

My driver was happily expounding upon the joys of his night before, but I wasn't listening. I grunted politely now and then to slip him a quiver of apparent interest, but all I could think about was *him*.

I was certain he would terrify me. He had become a legend, a dark legend by force of his complete absence from the public eye. Everyone knew about him: elders invoked his name whenever something inexplicable occurred in their neighborhood; mothers kept their daughters at home after dark; children scared each other senseless in the streets before going home to dinner. I thought about what he looked like, what his voice sounded like, what he would say or not say, whether he would look at me or mutter incomprehensibilities the way many introverted criminals do. Yet somehow I could not reconcile the notion of this man as a criminal—he was a medical doctor.

My journalistic pride bubbled up from my gut. Doctor or no doctor, he murdered her, in her own house. *Overworked physician murders patient in cold blood*, I thought. But I just couldn't make myself believe it.

My editor had come across the original article in a back issue of a competing newspaper, if running a paper under a national umbrella of censorship can really be called competition. Printed in the year 1946 in a paper much more loyal to the *Generalissimo* and his cronies than ours, it was over two decades old, but my editor, possessed of a morbid sense of irony—and somewhat righteous rivalry—felt it would be a rather good idea to revisit the crime on the 21st anniversary of the murder, particularly since the girl had been 21 at the time of her death. *These things always make good stories,* he said when he gave me the assignment. *See if you can dig up something new, something shocking the other paper missed.*

Sure, I had said. *Something the National Press and Propaganda Agency would shut us down for.*

The tattered article trembled in my hand as my cab rumbled over the unfortunate streets of Madrid. I thought perhaps I should take another look at it, but I had read it already five times. So I kept staring at it, trying to imagine the features and character of this mysterious doctor who had captured the imagination and horror of all of Spain, at precisely the wrong time in her history.

A few minutes later the taxi cab jolted to a stop. An imposing residence stood just across the street. *That must be it.* The driver happily exited and ran around to open the door for me. It was just another morning run for him.

I would have liked more time to imagine the doctor.

I stepped out of the car, catching my coat in the door—and dropped the article on the wet pavement.

Reaching down to pick it up, I suddenly remembered. In my haste to leave the office, I had forgotten my tape recorder. *No matter,* I thought, *I'll do without it just like in the good old days.*

I stood up and dug into my jacket for my notebook. There was the address the editorial assistant had written down for me. I looked up at the house I was now standing in front of, alone in the drizzling rain. My driver had wasted no time in getting back to the warm comfort of his seat.

If there were any sort of plate or sign with the number of the house to confirm the accuracy of my present location, I certainly couldn't find it. Centuries of ivy had consumed the heavy stone walls, ceding only to the enormous front door and the windows. My only hope was that my driver knew where he was going; if I couldn't locate the number on the house standing directly in front of it, I didn't quite grasp how he could have done so out of the windows of a moving taxi.

I turned around to call out to him, but he'd already gone. I stood there in the rain wondering if he'd remember he's due back in two hours. I never could tell with Spanish taxi drivers—especially now, after the war.

The drizzle was beginning to soak through my jacket, light but annoying just enough to push me toward the front door—and my assignment. There, in front of me, a solid iron door knocker hung in defiance. So adamant it could almost speak. I stood for a few moments more.

The doctor had requested a special leave of absence from his cell for the interview, given that it would be, as he had assured my editor, his first and only interview to any paper since his incarceration. He refused to be interviewed in prison. Such a request would be impossible for most convicted criminals, but his reputation as a man of medicine far preceded him. They quietly made an exception.

This house was somehow chosen, by someone, as apparently discreet and secure enough to contain him.

Something moved. I shot a glance toward the corner of the residence. A shadow of a man in a heavy black suit slipped just out of sight. *Guards*, I thought. I thought it again, for peace of mind.

There was not a sign of life in the streets—as if everyone feared for the lives of their daughters...

Just then, the door pulled slowly open. A rather striking older woman, evidently the housekeeper of the place, stared at me accusingly, but let me in without a word. I stepped inside and hesitated, expecting her to lead me to the doctor's chambers, but she waited for me instead. Her dark olive complexion and jet-black hair despite her advanced years—I would have guessed early sixties—framed eyes not afraid to look right through you. She needed no words to express her will. But I was an American journalist with a mind of my own and an inbred habit of resisting implicit cultural nuances and expectations. My Spanish colleagues at the paper had a running bet on when I'd finally be apprehended by one authority or another.

I stared at her and she stared at me and I thought *by God if neither one of us moves we'll stand here forever.* So I took the first step, not out of capitulation but resolute determination, and walked head on into the darkness of the corridor, plunging into an odor of old rotting wood and dusty oil portraits and forgotten mold that had eaten into the crevices of antique knick knacks. My eyes not yet having adjusted to the utter blackness, my instinct told me to hold out my hand to guide me, but my ego dug in and I, unsure of my way, continued on with the woman of the house behind me, the two of us silently plodding along what seemed to be a corridor without end.

There was apparently a door somewhere ahead, for suddenly the housekeeper brushed past me and knocked on it. No answer came and none was needed; her knock was a mere formality. She led me inside. A solitary ray of light cut the room into pieces. In the far corner, a figure sat hunched over a desk.

There was no question who it was.

The doctor turned around with the first step I took.

And I, the most loquacious of journalists, found myself *sans mots*. Far from the unshaven, stark-eyed madman he had so often been painted to be in popular media, he was the epitome of the kind, wise family doctor you'd want to take all the kids in the neighborhood to see. Rich, jet-black hair that had resisted the stress of age and confinement, eyes warm with the compassion and knowing only true medical doctors possess, skin of rich olives ripened in the Spanish sun.

"Mr. ---," said the doctor. His voice was clear and sound and offered no evidence of latent insanity.

"Pleasure to meet you, doctor," I said. The doctor rose and held out his hand. I must have seemed rude, for I stared at it an instant. I took it and found it exceptionally warm, kind—if hands can be kind—and somehow understanding. I strained to see his face.

"I'm very pleased you could come," said the doctor, inviting me to a chair by his desk. "Do you need paper?"

"No, that's fine, thank you." I was struck by his demeanor.

"I'm sorry about the light," he smiled, picking up on my squint. "I'm so used to low light, you know"—and he paused emphatically—"but here, let me open the shades a bit so you can write."

He moved to the window and pulled the curtains aside. But I did not want to see to write—I wanted to see to see *him*.

He sat into his chair with a sigh and gazed at me at length. Solitude had carved her sadness deep into his face, but his skin, the rich Spanish olive skin, refused to give up its flavors, and his eyes shone brilliantly at me, reigning victorious above the sentence imposed on him by Law.

"Would you like something to drink? Tea perhaps?"

"I'm sorry? Oh—yes of course." He had taken me unawares—I was still staring at his face, because he was so completely unalike what I had imagined that I did in fact need the hot tea to come to my cold, calculated—and clearly wrongly informed—journalistic senses.

Later it struck me... I never drank tea, and neither did the Spanish!

The door opened then and the housekeeper came in bringing a tea set for two on an old silver tray. I marveled how fast he had managed to summon her and surmised she must have had the hot water already waiting.

The doctor took his tea with a sprinkling of dark sugar; I opted for honey. It was mint tea, fresh, aromatic, mesmerizing, served in colorful glasses I remembered from my days as a war correspondent in Morocco. He watched me calmly, with no impatience or judgment, and I had the sensation he was looking far into my past, into who I had been and who I was then, and perhaps much more—I felt he knew more about me than I did.

The tea seared its molten traces through my torso and into my stomach. I put down my glass and picked up my pen. The doctor held silent. For the first time in my professional life I didn't know how to begin an interview. So I decided to explain the obvious.

"I'm not here to reopen the case, sir," I began. I paused, but the doctor politely waited for me, his eyes warm and understanding. "I think everyone remembers essentially what happened, but the years have covered the details in hearsay and legends and I—"

The doctor waved his hand in a rather singular horizontal motion.

"What do you know about it, my son?"

The "son" made me self-conscious. I was too old to be his son.

"What I know is that you were accused of murdering the daughter of a prominent lawyer here in Madrid, that you maintain the killer was someone else and you were framed, and that you were sentenced to life in prison without much of a trial. A sentence later commuted to 25 years. That's about it."

The doctor nodded gravely.

"Everything you say is true. I was accused, I do so maintain, and I was sentenced," he replied cryptically. "But before you ask me your questions, let me tell you the story from the beginning. Do you have time? Yes of course you do, you're a journalist."

I didn't have time precisely because I was a journalist, but I could hardly refuse.

"You don't wish to record?" asked the doctor. Dismayed at his having uncovered my absentmindedness, I nonchalantly replied, "I prefer the old-fashioned way, by hand."

"Very well. I shall start at the beginning. Twenty-one years ago I was practicing medicine in Cordoba," the good doctor began. "I was teaching at the University in Granada at the same time, because my medical practice did not bring in much. You see, I could never accept payment for the services I rendered. Medical service is a necessity in life, and those unlucky enough to need it should not be required to pay—especially in times of hardship, which we all saw plenty of then. But"—he waved his hand in that unique way of his—"that is simply irrelevant here. One day I received a phone call from a colleague of mine in Madrid. Well, a colleague only by profession, because you see I never met this man."

"Never?" I said.

"Never. To this day I cannot tell you who this assumed physician was. He had a light accent that betrayed a foreign nationality. He asked me if I could come to Madrid right away on an urgent matter.

"I asked him, 'What could be so urgent that you must summon me? Do you not have doctors in Madrid?' He replied that I was being specifically asked for by Don ---. I had never heard the name and so could not pretend to be impressed. I told the man that I was sorry but that I simply could not get away from my work in Cordoba.

"He called again the next week, offering me large sums of money. I began to be annoyed with him and told him I don't practice medicine for money. It was then that his tone changed. He warned me in no uncertain language that if I did not come to Madrid within the week, I would not be practicing at all. I told him I do not tolerate threats and he can do what he will, but my practice is my practice, and the only way to stop me is to put a bullet in my head."

The doctor paused for a bit, the old memory of such an affront to his honor still capable of stirring his fury. I nodded respectfully, which seemed to relax him enough to go on.

"'Dr. ---,' the man said, 'You will not be the one to

pay for your indiscretion. Your family will.' He then proceeded to offer certain details about members of my family to prove the seriousness of his threat. I was, as you can imagine, quite concerned; I had managed to elude the White Terror in Andalusia, surely you remember those days... several of my colleagues, rest their souls, had not been so lucky. All I knew at that moment is that I simply could not risk the safety of my family—not even for the medical profession, or any insufferable political cause."

The doctor's jaw tightened as he spoke. I knew all too well the massacres he was referring to. I'd covered them.

"I arrived in Madrid the next day. I settled in at the hotel they had secured for me, a rather luxurious affair that may have impressed another man, but I was indifferent. Before dawn on the day following, I was taken to an estate somewhere in the north of the city."

"You said you never met the man who originally called you."

"No. There was only one other person in the car with me—the driver, and he never let me see his face. In all of the time I spent on this miserable engagement, he spoke to me only once, and acknowledged my daily greetings to him with nothing more than a light nod."

I thought drily of my driver. The two should get together for a drink.

"But to continue: it was just before dawn. As soon as the car came to a stop, my door was immediately and briskly opened and I was ushered out of the car and into the imposing residence. Inside, I found myself in a large foyer, with a marble floor, richly decorated walls, and a rather elegant staircase leading somewhere to the upper level.

"The man who had shown me in—and uttered only a short greeting, I should add—indicated I should head upstairs. Oh, how often I have thought of that flight of stairs!" The doctor trembled suddenly. "That cursed staircase that I thought breathtakingly beautiful the first time! It's as if I never descended. I was to climb that staircase many times, every day, just before dawn.

"At the top of the staircase was a door. It was a lovely wooden door, painted white. I assumed I was to open it— I was given no instructions, and so I relied on my own instincts to guide me.

"I opened the door without knocking. Inside was a plain whitewashed room with two French windows, also whitewashed. I stood in the doorway, waiting for my eyes to adjust, but presently there was no need. A shaft of light broke through the darkness then, for the sun had risen. Slowly the room began surrendering its secrets to me. One of those secrets was to be my end. Never was there a curse more beautiful than this..."—here the doctor lost his voice momentarily—"on a white feather bed lay a young girl—she couldn't have been more than twenty or perhaps twenty-one—apparently asleep. She was breathtaking. She had luxurious dark brown hair, skin like sun-ripe olives, her eyelashes the shape of angel's wings. Her breathing was nervous and short, as if she were suffering at that moment from some terrifying nightmare. But she was pale, very pale, too pale for someone of her age. I immediately knew this was the reason I had been summoned, and I knelt down to open my medical bag."

" 'The only child of a prominent Spanish lawyer, whose mysterious illness stupefied every doctor in Madrid,'" I quoted from memory from the newspaper article.

The doctor shook his head adamantly, gesturing with his hand in that characteristic horizontal motion of his.

"I have my own theories as to whether or not the family itself was Spanish. Who knows? Perhaps. I have conjured up thousands of theories since then, but in the end, none of them matters but the one that sets you free. Perhaps you know more than I about these matters." He paused for a bit. "Journalists usually do."

He looked searchingly at me, as if I could put an end to 21 years of questions thrown to the wind, 21 years of empty injustice never explained. Before I could respond, the doctor smiled. Something in his smile betrayed he knew more than he was telling.

"No matter. It is as it is. I did not wish to startle the girl, as she seemed to be wavering on that erratic edge between sleep and wakefulness; and so I sat down on a chair nearby and waited. The sun rose outside, filling the room with an overwhelming and brilliant light. I looked around the room and noticed that everything, from the walls to the furniture to the minimal decorations, was white or of a very muted, neutral color, and quite suddenly I felt an indescribable sense of calm, a profound tranquility, you know, the kind that hovers above the altars of churches and among the pews just after mass, when everyone has gone to return to their daily lives in that loud busy world outside, but you stay, you stay and you just listen to the old stone walls that have been consecrated to the Lord...."

The doctor's face had unconsciously relaxed, and his eyes, I saw, looked off into the distant past, a past that only he knew and that had saved him from losing his brilliant mind while his body languished in his cell.

A medical doctor and a pious man to boot, I thought. *Jailed for murder.* I held my judgment.

"I must have sat there on that chair for over an hour—I cannot be sure precisely how long, but I finally stood when I could no longer feel my legs. I walked to the window and looked outside. A splendid garden stretched on away from the house for nearly a city block. The roses alone could have filled the Royal Palace. In the distance I could discern a stone wall, and it appeared to be the same wall that I had passed through earlier—it evidently encircled the estate. I could not see much more than that—beyond the garden must have been a street, for there I could see the rooftops of houses.

"I stood gazing out the window for a few moments, and thought to open it, for the air was very stale and unhealthy—particularly for the girl. I carefully slid the latch up and turned it to open the window. At first it would not give; I wondered if perhaps it was because the room had been recently painted, or because it had never been opened. I had to employ a certain degree of force to break it open. The latch made a sharp crack, and immediately afterward there came a sudden sigh from the girl. Afraid I had caused her to waken suddenly, I quickly turned around, but she had merely moved her head.

"I pushed the window wide open to let the fresh air in and approached her bedside. She had turned her head toward the wall, her blanket falling aside a bit to reveal a number of marks on the inside of her arm that alarmed me. Faint, but unmistakable puncture wounds, as those of a medical needle, but one clearly handled by inexperienced hands. A light pink color betrayed slight inflammation around the entry points.

"Sufficiently alarmed, I decided not to wait any longer. I took out my customary medical equipment and made a few preliminary tests, taking care not to disturb her too much. Her vital signs were acceptable, but something was clearly wrong, to my sense very wrong indeed. I would need more time, and I would need to speak to her.

"Just at that moment the door opened and a man entered the room. I recognized him as the same man who had ushered me into the house. He was tall and broad-shouldered, with a thick head of raven black hair, an olive skin, and exuded power and authority. Perhaps his most outstanding feature was his well-trimmed moustache. I thought perhaps he was the mysterious caller who had summoned me here, but was soon proven wrong when he spoke—for it was not the same voice.

"'Good morning, doctor. Thank you for coming on such short notice,'" he said.

" 'Good morning,' I said, not sure if I should be so bold as to ask his name since he had not offered it. But before I could say another word, he said, "'I am sorry but you must go now. She must rest.'

"I protested that I had just begun my examination,

whereupon he insisted, 'You will continue tomorrow.' I protested again: this girl was evidently in need of a thorough examination and proper treatment for whatever it was that was ailing her—moreover, I had been summoned, I told the man, under threat to my own family, something I did not take lightly.

"At this point the man came close to the bedside where I stood and looked sternly at me. 'You will continue tomorrow,' he repeated, his voice cold and hard. He then saw that the window had been opened and his eyes flittered with rage. He briskly stepped over to the window, closed it with a sudden gentleness and caution, and said, 'Do not ever touch anything in this room that you do not require for your examination.'

"I once again protested that the air in the room was very stale and that the girl needed fresh air, but the man ushered me rather impolitely out of the room. He closed the door firmly behind us and I, blocked by him, was forced to descend. He remained standing at the top of the stairs as if to make certain I would not attempt to reenter the room.

"I was so shaken by the morning's events that it did not occur to me to try to get a good idea of the rest of the house. I found myself outside somehow, remembered the front gate, and there, as if by clockwork, I found the car waiting. Just then I came back to my senses. What sort of father—or family member, or whatever sort of responsible guardian—was a man who turns away a doctor his family had gone to so much trouble to secure for their daughter?

"I turned back around, firmly intending to go back to the girl's room and demand to see her, but the front door had already been locked! I looked for a doorbell but there was none. Nor a door knocker of any kind. I resorted to knocking as loudly as I could with my knuckles, then my fists. The house remained obstinately silent. I expected the man to come bounding out of the house with a pack of hunting dogs for all the noise I made, but nothing. The driver, who was waiting in the car, did not react, did not come out and what is more, never seemed to take any notice of anything I did, not that first morning or any other thereafter.

"The next day I was driven to the house again under cover of night. Again the driver said nothing, again I was ushered hurriedly into the house, up the elegant staircase and through the door painted white. Again the day dawned white and brilliant, filling the room with an angelic aura; the girl was sleeping soundly. I earnestly desired to bring her back to health, but above all to protect her from the demons that inhabited her house. I could only assume the broad-shouldered man was somehow related to her, for I had no reason to assume otherwise."

The doctor paused for a moment, allowing himself the memory of that angelic aura he spoke of, as if it might break the nightmare and bring him back to his youth—and his freedom, which I imagined he valued even more.

"I could not make this man—whom I shall call 'master of the house' if you will allow me, as I never did learn his name—understand that I needed to examine the girl while she was awake. He seemed to be possessed by a violent desire to bring her back to health—and fast—and yet he interfered with the very process necessary to do so! I fought him as well as I knew how, used every psychological device, every tactic, threat, and trick, but nothing moved this man. He was deaf to everything except requests for specific medical supplies.

"I had two hours every morning starting with the first light of dawn, and not a second more. I could not know whether she was awake during the day and simply slept long in the mornings, or whether her sleep had been artificially induced to prevent me from speaking to her. Despite the pain it caused me, I was forced to conclude that I could do nothing for the girl, given the extremely restrictive conditions of my examination.

"I determined to submit a medical report and return home at the end of the week. I considered this situation, this game this man or this family played, unusually cruel and without logic, and wanted no part in it. I did not, of course, tell them of my design. I simply examined the girl every morning as I was told, gave my daily observations, which did not, naturally, change, and planned my escape.

"That Saturday morning, everything was the same. I mounted the long winding staircase to the girl's bedroom, attended her for two hours, and was then shown out by the master of the house. The driver drove me to the hotel, I thanked him as usual, and went upstairs to my room. I had every intention to take my bag, which I had prepared the night before, and board the next train to Cordoba. But that morning something awaited me that changed my plans. A sealed envelope lay on the bed. Puzzled, I opened it. For a moment I fancied it was the explanation to this ridiculous game, and hoped that they, whoever they were, had had a good laugh at my expense, that the girl was perfectly healthy and had merely played along, and I could now go home. Instead, I found a 1,000-peseta note and a letter. The letter intrigued me far more than the money."

The letter piqued my curiosity as well, although the money—for a week's work—certainly wasn't anything to cast aside. I thought briefly about my journalist's salary.

"What did it say?" I asked.

"It ran a little like this: 'Dear Dr. ---, we wish to express our most profound gratitude to you for having agreed to come such a long way to attend to our daughter. She is our most precious treasure, the only thing in this world that gives us joy in our otherwise desperate lives. Enclosed in this letter you will find a small token of our most deeply felt appreciation. We hope you will find it in your heart to stay just a few more weeks and attend to our daughter. She already seems to be getting better, and we believe she will come out of this illness fresher than a spring rose, may the Lord permit it to be so.'"

"Was the letter signed?" I interjected.

"It was, but the signature was illegible."

"Hmm." I noted this. "What did you do?"

"I did what any self-respecting doctor would do. I stayed. Not for the money, mind you, for money means nothing to me. I sent it all to my wife in Cordoba. I stayed because I was beginning to suspect something other than an ill-spirited game. She clearly was the daughter, perhaps the only child, of someone who cared for her deeply; after this letter I began to doubt that her father could be the gentleman I saw every morning, as I had thought previously, for the tone of the letter did not match his demeanor. I was determined to save the girl, who was evidently the victim of some sort of foul play. I was equally determined to uncover whatever crime was being committed and report it to the authorities. I decided to conduct a few non-medical tests.

"The next morning I followed their protocol to the letter, although I took care not to stray too far from my customary demeanor so as not to call attention to my actions. But I carried with me a few extra tools I had procured that prior afternoon: a little bag of powdered paprika, a drip-can of gray paint I had tightly wrapped in wool, a rubber band, a needle, and a spool of white thread.

"A few moments after I organized myself in the young girl's room as I usually did, I loosened the collar of her nightgown slightly and patted the paprika onto her cheeks and neck, making her appear quite flushed. I practiced my emotional state—"

The doctor paused, noticing my raised eyebrow.

"What I mean to say, is that my countenance and body language had to match the apparent urgency I needed to express. I was no actor, but my body and mind knew all too well the psychological imprint of a true medical concern. Mimicking it for the sake of this young girl seemed to me an insignificant price for the dignity of my profession. Would you not agree?"

I nodded, sufficiently impressed with the doctor's inner moral compass not to question his motives.

"I then firmly took hold of the bedroom door handle, opened the door, and started down the stairs, my face registering the resolute expression of a doctor desperately looking for a cold compress. In reality I was, of course, on a keen look-out. I reached the bottom of the stairs without encountering a soul but, because I had never seen any other part of the house, was then unsure of where to go. I chose a hallway that seemed to lead further into the house, and followed it for a few meters until it opened up into a luxurious sitting room. The walls were papered in an intricate gold print reminiscent of old mosques; an exquisite crystal chandelier hung from the ceiling over a polished black grand piano. A marble fireplace emitted a welcome warmth with its low fire, evidently recently attended to.

"Just then a voice snapped at me: 'What are you doing here? Should you not be upstairs tending to Isabella?' I turned around, concealing my joy at having unexpectedly discovered the name of the girl. It was the master of the house, visibly furious.

" 'I'm sorry, sir, I didn't hear you. What did you say?' I purposely made the man think I had failed to hear the name. He had naturally realized his mistake, so he relaxed somewhat when I did not let on I'd heard the name. He changed his reply slightly, no doubt thinking himself quite clever: 'I said, what are you doing here, doctor? You should be upstairs.'

" 'Yes, of course,' I replied. 'But the girl seems to have flared up suddenly and I need a cold compress to cool her down.'

" 'You should have pulled the cord,' he said.

" 'I did, my good man. There was no response, and this is a rather urgent matter.' I answered firmly.

"He frowned. 'I'll have it sent up right away.' Without another word I brushed quickly past him and back up the staircase, keeping up my role as the worried doctor, so as not to give him any more reason for suspicion.

"Upstairs, I continued to tend to the girl—*Isabella! Isabella!* I kept repeating her name to myself so I would never forget it—as if she were burning up with fever. Presently there was a knock at the door. 'Come in,' said I, expecting the master of the house to open the door. Instead, a woman entered. She was dressed in the garb of a maid and had a dark olive complexion, jet-black hair, and facial features rather typical of Arab women. I would have said she was, possibly, in her forties—for, as you know, it can be near impossible to guess a woman's age, and certainly dangerous! On a silver tray she bore the cold compress I had asked for. I took the compress and said, 'shokran,' the Arabic word for 'thank you.'

"The woman started, evidently not expecting me to

speak to her in her own language. She looked searchingly at me, a dark, fiery, but suppressed rage in her eyes unsure whether to hate or fear me. 'La shokra ala wajib,' she said quickly, bowed, and left the room.

"This was all very strange indeed, and I found myself even further away from solving the mystery than I had hoped for earlier that morning. Nevertheless, I was determined to succeed. I carefully wiped the paprika from Isabella's cheeks and neck and set to work. I threaded the needle I had brought with me and sewed a small cross into the underside of one of the corners of the uppermost bed sheet, and then connected a loose thread from the blanket to her pillow, leaving enough room between the two for normal movement during sleep. I sprinkled a little of the paprika into the right corner of her mouth, but ever so little as to be completely unnoticeable.

"I had one more task to carry out before my allotted two hours passed. I took a sheet of paper from my prescription pad and scrawled across it as illegibly as I could a simple prescription for a remedy typically used to treat mild fever and congestion. I then pulled on the cord next to the bed, which normally summoned the master of the house whenever I needed something, but to my surprise, the maid entered once again. I had to think quickly.

"I told her, in Arabic to make sure she followed my instructions to the word, to deliver this prescription to her master and that he fill it with the utmost urgency. The maid repeated the Arabic word for 'prescription,' 'wassfa,' carefully, as if she wished to ascertain that this was in fact what I was saying. It struck me that she should react with such caution to a routine medical procedure—a prescription—and more, that she should appear to question my authority. I sternly commanded her to do my bidding, lest I summon the master of the house, whereupon she fell defiantly silent and did as told."

As fresh as if it had been yesterday, the memory of this particular incident flashed fierce and hot over the kind doctor's countenance.

"Yet when he came upstairs to ask me what I had written, precisely as I had planned—hence the illegible scrawl, you understand—I saw that it was not my writing. Someone had re-written my prescription on a different piece of paper!"

"I do not follow, doctor. It had to be the same. You had just written it on your prescription pad," I exclaimed. "I doubt they had one of their own in the house."

The doctor waved his hand again with his characteristic gesture.

"My prescription pad has a section of blank pages. I had written the prescription on one of these by sheer accident, never dreaming that someone would rewrite it. But it was an accident that would quickly prove fortuitous. You see, the paper that the master of the house held in his hand was of a different size. I could tell because I pay great attention to detail; you really must do so if you consider yourself an attentive physician.

"That was, in fact, what gave away the falsified prescription. Not the writing. Whoever rewrote my prescription, had an exceedingly faithful hand, to the point where I myself may not have been able to catch it if the paper had been the same size."

"Even with your attention to detail, as you have just said?" I ventured. Despite my profound interest in the doctor's story, I still retained the cool head of an investigative journalist: I wondered if I had perhaps caught the doctor in his first deception.

"The kind of attention to detail a physician must have, and employ on a daily basis, is not quite the same as that of an editor—or a journalist," the doctor replied, his gaze boring firm yet warm into mine, reminiscent of a father patiently teaching his son the ways of the world.

"It makes use of all the senses, and takes a great many more variables from the outside world into context—so the physician can tell, for example, whether a patient's flushed cheeks are the result of an excessively warm bed or a fever stemming from a dangerous infection. And so I would naturally note the size or shape of a prescription note first, before the more minute details of handwriting."

I was effectively disarmed, to my personal relief.

"To continue, then: I took the note from the man's hand and gazed at it for some time, an expression of great concern on my face. I then looked at him, shook my head, and said precisely what you've just observed: 'This is not the prescription I sent down.'

"He looked at me as if I were mad.

" 'Who sent it, if not you?' he said. 'The maid brought it down to me directly.'

" 'Then I'm afraid the only one who could have rewritten it is she, sir,' I said.

" 'She is illiterate, doctor.'

"I did not believe him. I did not believe her, either—I did not know whom to believe, and had no other recourse but to play them off against each other until a crack appeared somewhere in the impossible armor of this nightmare.

" 'Whether or not she is illiterate, sir, it may behoove you to watch her a bit more closely,' I told him as meaningfully as I could. 'I certainly have no interest in rewriting my own prescriptions.'

"This seemed to have the desired effect on him—at least sufficient enough for him to do just as I had hoped he would: write the prescription down himself as I dictated, so that I could see his handwriting, which had been my design all along."

"But see his handwriting for what reason?" I was not following. The doctor leaned forward to explain.

"Put yourself in my position, my son. Your family has been threatened. You find yourself in a strange house full of strange people, ordered to attend a girl you are to cure only while she sleeps. So to ensure your safety and that of your own family, you are forced to act according to the situation, regardless of how inexplicable that situation may be. His handwriting would perhaps offer a clue into the bizarre mystery I had found myself entangled in.

"To continue, then: I spelled out for the master of the house precisely the medicine I wanted, watching closely over his shoulder as he wrote. You see, I needed to know if he had written that letter of thanks that had been delivered to my hotel room. But the handwriting was not the same. Whoever wrote the letter, according to my observation, was someone different. Therefore this man was not Isabella's father, but then who was? And what relation was he to her? I felt the answers to these questions would go a fair distance to release me from my predicament.

"Ironically, these very same answers have delivered me to where I am today," said the doctor, calmly, clearly having accepted his fate some time ago, and dropped off into thought.

I had been able to ask far too few questions. I was already tempted to convince myself of the doctor's innocence; most of the questions I had had, he naturally addressed in his narrative. But I had to remain objective and hear his story through to the end.

"Did you ever discover who he was and who was this family?" I asked, my tone strictly professional.

The doctor gestured me to be patient.

"Wait, my good fellow, wait. Let me finish the story. Still burning with a repressed rage, the master of the house drily thanked me and brusquely exited the room, prescription in hand. I waited until his footsteps carried him well down along the staircase, and ventured outside the room onto the landing, leaning over the staircase as far as I could to follow the events which were about to ensue.

"There in the sitting room below, broke out a controlled but violent explosion of fury—an argument between him and the maid, judging by the sound of the two voices engaged in the exchange. I could discern very few words, for the conversation, if it could be called that, was too far away to hear clearly, but the words that I did pick up were all in Arabic. It became clear then that he was either of Arab origin, or at least spoke the language, for his features were not immediately recognizable as Arab.

"I then heard footsteps and quickly slipped back behind the bedroom door. I thought breathlessly, what should I take up to appear busy and there, on the small writing desk by the bed, I saw the piece of paper—the forged prescription—that the man had brought up with him; I had almost forgotten it. I put it into the pocket of my medical coat, and in the nick of time, for the door opened immediately afterward: it was the master of the house, calm and composed, informing me it was time to go. I noted a distinct change in his voice: it was softer, more careful. I sensed he did not wish to threaten me.

"I gathered my medical bag, glancing inside to confirm my 'extra' supplies were all still in order, and stopped just once more by the bedside of young Isabella who had been momentarily forgotten in all the commotion. As I bent down to touch her forehead, I checked to ensure my handiwork with the threaded pillow and blanket had not been detected. I then left the room, actively scratching my head, looking extremely worried and pretending to be lost in thought. My acting once again had a visible effect on the master of the house—the effect I desired. He accompanied me down the stairs, something he had never done before.

" 'What is the matter, doctor?' I pretended at first not to pay any attention to him, and only a few seconds later exclaimed, 'I beg your pardon? Oh, I'm sorry, I was thinking about the girl. It seems to be a little more serious than I had thought.'

"This made the man nervous. He stopped me just before the front door. 'Did you receive payment yesterday?' he asked. I immediately saw an opportunity to disconcert him further. 'Yes, thank you, I did. But perhaps next time you could arrange for safer transport of the money.'

" 'I'm afraid I do not follow.'

" 'The envelope had been opened,' I said, quite uncomfortable with telling a lie, but reassured myself it was all for the sake of Isabella. 'Whoever opened it then tried to seal it again, but failed to cover his traces. I do believe the amount was correct, but I would prefer a sealed envelope. You understand.' I placed a grave emphasis on those last two words.

" 'Of course,' he said, visibly disturbed. I bid him goodbye and headed for the front gate where my car was waiting as usual. He stood in the doorway looking after me, deep in thought. Inside the car, I quickly transferred the drip can, the rubber band, and my note pad from my medical bag into the pockets of my coat, then waited for the driver to start the engine and move perhaps a few meters. I then emitted a slight gasp.

" 'Oh!' I exclaimed. 'Please hold on a moment, I think I may have dropped my note pad by the front gate.' The driver hesitated, craning his neck to look back toward the house, but only slowed the car.

" I insisted. 'My good man, please have the courtesy to stop the car. That pad has all of my medical notes in it; I'm certain you'd like nothing to do with their loss.'

"With that, the driver visibly shook, betraying that same strange ice-cold fear that had paralyzed the master of the house with the incident of the false prescription.

"Turning around again to ensure no one could see, he reluctantly stopped the car, and nervously motioned with his head for me to go. I exited, walked around to the back, and bent down near the car's tail pipe. I quickly produced the drip-can from my wide coat pocket and affixed it to the exhaust with the large rubber band so that the paint would drip at more or less regular intervals."

"Were you not concerned, doctor," I said, "that the can of paint would overheat during the drive?"

"Ah, that was the purpose of the wool I had wrapped around the drip-can," replied the doctor. "Wool of course burns, but the drive was far too short for it to ignite. Nylon would have been safer, but nearly impossible to obtain within a single day. As for the paint," he said, anticipating my next question, "it was a light gray, intended to blend with the natural hue of the road when dry, and water-based, which meant the next rain would wash it away.

The doctor looked at me, waiting for any other questions. "Fair enough, please go on," I said.

"I then took the note pad from my pocket to bring into the car with me, but I dare say it was unnecessary, for the driver never turned to look at anything I did. I had barely closed the passenger-side door when he stepped hard on the accelerator, the car jolting as it took off.

"I waited about halfway through the ride—just as we were approaching a curve in the road—and wound down my window, something I had never done before. The driver noticed immediately, but because he was driving, could not fully turn his head. As I said before, he spoke to me only once in the entire engagement, and it was during that morning's drive back to the hotel.

" 'I am sorry but they not like window open,' he said, his voice slow and his accent broken."

" 'They'?" I interrupted. "Did the master of the house have an accomplice perhaps?"

The doctor looked at me, searching for himself in my eyes.

"That single sentence was the first ray of light in this impossible period of darkness. It gave me two important clues: one, that it was more than one person, which I could assume to be either Isabella's family or another group of individuals bound by some dark interest; and two, if they were able to dictate, remotely no less, such insignificant details as whether the window of the car was open or not, they were not a trivial force. Whoever was behind this depravity, exercised enough power and influence that neither resources nor the law were of any concern."

Or, for that matter, the regime itself, I thought. The self-installed national government left no social stone unturned in their ruthless hunt for dissidents; and once found, they were hastily and often brutally done away with. Unless, of course, their political or business connections afforded them some measure of protection, and then the procedure of eliminating them became all that more careful and complex—but no less ruthless. I sensed the doctor and I shared similar sentiments on this point—but that would need to remain forever unspoken... for both our sakes.

My tea had long since grown cold, forming that thin skin of tannin that teas usually do when left standing too long. I had lost all sense of time, and the windows refused to betray any hint of what time of day it was.

I looked at my notes. I had filled several pages already, enough to write a short novel. The doctor followed my gaze, and gave a short but hearty laugh, the first and only of our entire interview.

"Wonderful, my good man, wonderful." He slapped the large wooden desk. "I'm glad this story of mine has caught your attention, and held it for so long. It's held *me* for much longer," he added, his words heavy with a dark humor only he could appreciate.

"I'm sorry, doctor," I said.

"Whatever for?"

"I'm a journalist. I interview, I observe, I gather and analyze facts, and then I report. I'm not sure how I can possibly write this story without calling for a re-opening of the case."

The doctor waved his hand.

"It's far too late for that. My allotted time in prison will soon end. I would prefer not to stir the hornet's nest, if you understand my meaning."

"You could be freed sooner," I protested. "You *should* be, if you are indeed innocent. There is no greater injustice than keeping an innocent man in prison."

"Ah, but there is. There is," he said. "And that is the painfully protracted process of 'law enforcement' here in Spain. What you suggest may take years, and quite easily more years than what is left in my sentence."

Not being Spanish myself, but having lived in this country through much of her recent pain and horror, I knew full well the import of the doctor's words. Spain had forged her reputation with the blood of her own sons and daughters, and dragged her honor through the mud of political convenience and moral hypocrisy. And as any persona carrying an excess of her own importance, she was bloated with a blind and incompetent bureaucracy—its clerks and administrators made Don Quixote look like a professor of nuclear physics.

"Would you like me to continue, or do you need to attend to other pressing matters?"

"Please continue, doctor," I said, "if you have the time." As soon as I uttered the words, I clenched my teeth, chastising myself for being so insensitive. But the doctor simply smiled: "I do have the time. But here, let's get you some more hot tea—" and he called out to the housekeeper who in just a few moments appeared with a fresh glass of that wonderful aromatic nectar.

"Now where was I... ah yes. Emboldened by my driver's fear of his employers, I brazenly ignored him. I angled my stethoscope mirror out the window so that I could see whether the drip-can was fulfilling its duty. As we turned the curve, I could indeed distinguish an irregular gray line following us. Satisfied, I sat back and relaxed, I dare say, for the first time since my arrival in Madrid.

"My driver insisted: 'You must close window, please.'

" 'I beg your pardon?' I said, under the pretense I had not heard him the first time. 'I cannot open the windows of this vehicle to breathe a bit of fresh air? For the love of the good Lord. Who is the person I need to speak to to tell them how ridiculous this demand is?'

"The silence I was met with upon my request spoke, as they say, volumes. He was, I hypothesized, under the direct employment of the same people who had hired the man I called the 'master of the house'."

"But how could you be sure, doctor?" I said. "What if the 'master of the house' were indeed the girl's father, perhaps locked in some kind of conflict or lawsuit with these people? He certainly seemed, from what you have told me thus far, to be quite passionate about Isabella's condition, even if he was a bit temperamental."

"Certainty is a relative concept, my son," the doctor said, "in law, in medicine, and in crime. Events I am about to disclose to you confirmed my hypothesis beyond any reasonable doubt.

"To continue then: my driver continued for a while longer on his route in a dark and heavy silence that he presently broke with 'It is for your good and safety, sir. Please close window.'

" 'Very well,' said I, and rolled up my window. I had fulfilled my objective of confirming the paint was marking our route, so I had no further reason to stress the poor lad. The rest of the journey passed by without incident.

"When we arrived at my hotel, I bid the driver good day as I did every day, but purposely exited the car in as clumsy a fashion as I could muster without appearing too obvious. I needed a bit of time to remove the drip can from the exhaust, and so I used my very effective guise of the absent-minded doctor. I 'tripped' on my coat as I stepped out, and dropped my note pad close to the back wheel, which then of course obliged me to leave the car door open and kneel down to retrieve the pad—and pull the drip can off the tail pipe. I then stood up, muttering a stream of appropriate frustrations, and brushed myself off near the open door so the driver could see and hear me. Finally, I made it a point to peer inside the car and bid the driver good day once more—this entire show was, of course, to ascertain that he suspected nothing.

"Moments later, after the car had gone, I took my bicycle—as it happened, I had bought one several days prior from a young lad I'd seen on the street near the hotel who'd been trying to sell it for food. It kept me from going stark mad, being shut up in either the hotel or the house all day long—and followed the jagged gray line the can of paint had made. It was imperative that I do so immediately, for traffic and rain would have soon rubbed away most of the traces. It took me a good twenty minutes to wind my way back to the house. I noted the street address and number and cycled about a bit to get a general sense of the neighborhood."

"The address, doctor," I said quickly, "do you still remember it?"

"As clearly as if it had been yesterday," the doctor sighed. "Calle --- 32. It was a wealthy neighborhood, one of the most affluent areas of Madrid. This was no surprise to me—judging by the sums of money I was paid every week and the interior of the sitting room, I could only assume the family was very well off. Their financial status also aligned perfectly with the level of influence they very clearly held over the people in their employ—and, I am sorry to add, with the nature of their 'professional' relationship with them, which was, as we have seen, anything but congenial and supportive.

"It was critical to know the address, but also I needed to know the last name of the family. It is, as you can imagine, against all of my principles to steal or to lurk about private premises"—and here it struck me how mercilessly ironic the Law really was, Spanish or otherwise—"but the desire to save Isabella was stronger than any of these principles.

"And so I, a well-respected, licensed doctor of medicine, approached the mailbox like a common thief, looking about to make sure no one was observing me, and slid my pen underneath the rain cover of the box, carefully lifting it. There, in muted gold lettering, was the name ---. I had heard the name somewhere before... and then I remembered. Of course! The man who had telephoned me had said that my services were being requested by a Don ---, but I had not assigned any particular relevance to the name then. I wrote it in my note pad, and sped away as quickly as I could.

"The next morning, I nearly bounded up the stairs, pushing open the bedroom door with a great sense of expectation. Isabella was there in bed, as usual, but what interested me was to know whether the thread I had affixed the morning prior was still in its place. I closed the door behind me quietly and pressed my ear against it to make sure the man had not followed, and then carefully approached Isabella."

The doctor stopped to take a sip of his tea that surely had gotten quite cold. It did, and he called out to the housekeeper to refill his glass. She did so with her usual speed, and as she poured the steaming amber liquid into the glass, she smiled warmly at the doctor, placing her strong hand on his shoulder as if to protect him from nosy journalists. He nodded to her in thanks, relaxing in her presence—but he'd stopped at a rather inconvenient point in his narrative.

"You've got me hanging," I said.

"I was hanging myself then," he said. The bitter irony of his words was not lost on either one of us.

"What I didn't know that morning is that the little white thread I had sewn between her pillow and her blanket would become a noose, never tight enough to end my misery, yet never loose enough to let me go. But no matter—let us go on."

—I wasn't about to stop him—

"The thread, unbroken, was affixed precisely in the same manner as I had left it the day before. I checked Isabella's cheeks: they were as pale as before. I then touched the corner of her lips—the paprika was gone, wiped completely away. This led me to deduce, to my great relief, that Isabella had indeed eaten or been fed at least once since my departure the day prior, and that this had most likely been the pattern certainly since my assignment began, and perhaps earlier. Yet the unbroken thread contradicted that hypothesis: how could she eat, or be fed, with the thread still intact? I examined it again.

"To my great shock, I saw my thread had in fact been cut, and another had been sewn in its place. Care had been taken to sew another thread, of the same color, in the same position on both pillow and blanket. Only a small piece of the original thread remained attached at the little cross I had made on the corner of the blanket—and that is what, upon my closer examination, betrayed the duplicate handiwork."

The doctor voiced my own thoughts: "I instinctively thought of the maid, whom I already suspected of rewriting my prescription, for who else in this household had access to Isabella, and who else would exhibit this same level of attention to detail?

"But the larger question remained: why? Why take such great pains to replicate my work? I could not tell whether it was to protect or mislead me. As you can well imagine, the implications of these two diverging hypotheses were equally excruciating."

The doctor's very own Scylla and Charybdis, I thought. I was beginning to see a little deeper into the impossible web the doctor had fallen into. But not deep enough.

"If it was to mislead, you would have a strong case to plead your innocence," I ventured.

"As I said... I am beyond that now. Time has rendered my role in this wretched story irrelevant.

"You know, in medicine, a variety of observations and tests need to be conducted before a diagnosis can be made—I imagine it's not too different in your profession. One critical element, my inability to speak to Isabella or anyone who knew her medical history, was compounded by another: why she was so profoundly asleep each morning, so profoundly that none of the examinations I ever performed awakened her? The answer, for me as a physician, lay in the puncture marks on the inside of her arm. And so I examined them once again. One seemed fresher than the others—suggesting a recent injection. Of what drug or substance, I could not ascertain without proper testing, but at that point it became all too clear.

"The realization of the situation—Isabella's condition and my predicament—now struck me full force. I sat down wearily at her bedside, watching the unfortunate young thing. You see, Isabella was in a deep state of unconsciousness."

"A coma," I said.

"Yes, a coma. Now, this explained why she was always asleep when I arrived, but it also revealed the cynical mind that had set my doctor's hours to the early morning—to create the appearance of sleep rather than a coma. Given that she had moved, or been moved, at least enough to eat and perhaps even to get out of bed on a daily basis, I conjectured that the coma was intermittent and unnatural—in other words, induced.

"Twenty years ago, we in the medical field knew far less about states of unconsciousness than we do today, and some rather crude medical practices evolved. My great concern now was that Isabella was the victim of one of these experiments. Alas, coma was not my specialization! But as her only attending physician—to my knowledge—I needed to know at the very minimum, the basic facts. If my hypothesis was correct and indeed coma was being induced on a daily basis, what was the underlying condition that the coma was meant to ameliorate or stop? What drug was being used to induce it? Had there been an accident or was there something much more serious going on? All of these questions seared feverish tracks through my mind as I sat by Isabella's side, sick at the thought of having spent so many days unaware of her unconsciousness.

"The greatest error, in my estimation, that these people committed was hiring the wrong doctor."

"I would venture that your reputation for healing some of the most persistent ailments of the members of several well-to-do families had something to do with their decision," I said.

The doctor looked into my eyes incredulous. Yes, I had done my research.

"I never think about money when practicing my profession, as you know. I am a doctor, and a true doctor heals. This is a basic human service and a profession, not a business. This is why we take the Hippocratic Oath! Nevertheless, I am no novice when it comes to the caprices of the human ego. Perhaps I would have indeed been better off not to have made such an enviable name for myself. But, it is as it is," said the doctor, waving his past away with that characteristic motion of his.

"To continue, then: my very first instinct upon the discovery of Isabella's state, was to have a rather frank talk with the master of the house, but I needed a strategy, to protect Isabella in case he was in some way involved. Just then, in the midst of the fury raging inside me, there came a knock at the door.

" 'Yes,' I said heatedly. The door opened, and the master of the house came in with a silver tray.

" 'The medicine you ordered yesterday, doctor,' he said, putting the tray down on the bedside table.

" 'Thank you sir. And the maid? Will she be available for me?' I asked as nonchalantly as I could muster. The master of the house pressed his lips together, clearly in no mood to discuss her. Something was different about his demeanor that morning; he seemed quite on edge.

" 'It's best that she not disturb you, doctor. Whatever you need, I will attend to.' His unexpected diplomacy seemed out of place. I decided there and then to go on the offensive, and interrogate.

" 'Has she been with you long?' I asked. The man looked searchingly at me.

" 'Some time. Why do you ask?'

" 'Who takes care of this girl when I'm not here?' I demanded. To my surprise, the master of the house did not exhibit the violent temper I was expecting.

" 'The maid, but this is only very basic care—'

"I quickly interrupted: 'Food?' I said imperiously. Taken aback by my outburst, the master of the house replied on impulse—my goal precisely!

" 'Yes.'

" 'Water?'

" 'Yes.'

" 'Personal needs?' I pressed on, not giving him time to think.

"Here he hesitated, clearly out of respect for the privacy of a young girl. He looked at Isabella, and for the very first time, his features relaxed, into what I would go so far as to call a kind and compassionate gaze, yet one that was infused with an immense and profound sadness. But as he looked back at me, that gaze quickly hardened again.

" 'The maid provides basic care, doctor. As for her illness, you are the only qualified medical specialist. That is why we sent for you. We are not doctors and would not know what to do.'

"My confrontation paid off. He confirmed several crucial facts: one, that Isabella was indeed being fed and cared for, at least on a basic level; two, that there was indeed a group of people behind the curtain, as it were—he did say '*we* are not doctors.' And three, someone, *someone,* whoever it was in all of this strange affair, was not interested in nursing Isabella back to health, for otherwise they would have given me *carte blanche* for anything I needed."

"Would you be able to say, doctor," I said, "who in this group of persons that *someone* might be, whether or not you know their name?" I was careful not to lead the doctor on, as the ethics of journalism dictate.

"Oh, you mean the master of the house?" The good doctor knew a thing or two about human psychology. "If you had asked me that question in the first few days of my assignment, I would have vehemently said 'yes.' But his fleeting yet profound glance at Isabella confirmed what I had begun to suspect for some time: he was operating under extreme duress, and to a large degree against his will. He was no medical doctor, there was no doubt there; he really was completely lost as to what to do; otherwise, I would posit, he would have done it. But whoever was pulling the cords behind the scenes, did so with an iron hand that carried some sort of terrifying weapon—whether psychological, financial, or physical, was beyond my powers of conjecture."

Somehow, I doubted that. Somewhere, deep in my journalist's gut, I could tell he knew more today than he did 21 years ago.

"To continue, then," said the doctor, taking a sip of his tea. "I pressed on: 'Your maid, sir, does not fulfill her duties. This girl has not been eating well. Her sheets have not been changed—'

" 'Regardless,' interrupted the master of the house, having finally lost his patience. His voice betrayed the habitual fury he had been repressing. 'I would prefer to avoid any future misunderstandings, especially as far as prescriptions are concerned. I have therefore given the maid strict orders not to interfere with your work.'

"Underneath the fury, I could feel a nervous panic he was trying very hard to conceal. I aimed to exacerbate it.

" 'I'm afraid, sir, that we will have to take the girl to a hospital for intensive care—otherwise' and here I dealt my strongest card—'she may never recover from the coma.'

"Upon hearing the word 'coma,' the master of the house grew pale. This confirmed for me that he had had not the slightest idea as to what was being done to Isabella and, just as his glance at her moments ago had done, that he was sufficiently capable of compassion and emotionally invested in her to be fearful for her life. As well he should be, I say! I held him in utter disdain—him and the lot of them, whoever these people were. I cared nothing who was innocent and who wasn't, in the eyes of the Law; they were all guilty by association of endangering this innocent young girl's life.

"Just as their lot endangered so many other innocent lives," the doctor added, the first and only time he made any reference to the reigning monsters of Spain.

"But, sadly, not even the life of the young and the innocent could sway the fate that hovered over this house. The master of the house, despite himself, had no will power of his own.

" 'Impossible,' he told me. 'We don't have time.'

" 'Time for what?' said I, now furious myself. 'You, as the father, who evidently have a significant amount of financial resources at your disposal, should spare nothing to save your own daughter! *Haram alayk!*

"The man shook involuntarily at this. I doubt he had expected me to speak Arabic—I had, in fact, used the language for this purpose—and could not conceal his shock.

" 'I am not her father,' he muttered softly, in Castilian. 'But you must save her. Without hospitals. I will arrange whatever is necessary, provide you with whatever supplies you need, but no hospitals.'

" 'Then you will lose her. Without hospital care, she will die.'

"The man's face reddened. He moved his jaw as if he wished to utter a word, but he only managed to grunt threateningly. We stood there, he and I, glaring at each other, our separate furies lashing out at each other. I, as the doctor, stood my ground. Isabella was my patient, and I alone answered for her. The master of the house knew that on on these grounds his position was the weaker. Unable to force his hand, he turned around and walked out of the room. It was to be the last I would ever see of him.

"As I stood there alone in the room, adrenaline still gushing, I heard a piercing cry downstairs. Not a scream, but a cry, a long, drawn-out cry... a wail. Clearly a woman's voice. I slipped quickly out of the room and leaned over the railing at the top of the stairs.

"I was just in time—I caught sight of the maid running out of the kitchen quarters past the staircase, her hands covering her face, wailing as she ran. She disappeared around the corner that led into the sitting room. The master of the house then appeared, having apparently come after her. I deftly stepped aside into the shadow of the upper landing, lest he look up and catch me following the scene, but he lingered only a few moments, looking after her, before he retired back toward the direction of the kitchen quarters.

"I stood transfixed, my heart still racing but my mind numb. In the Arab culture, a wail is, as you well know, a sign of grief on the passing of a loved one. My full mental state was still with Isabella whom I had just discovered to be in a coma—imagine then the chill in my bones upon hearing this cry. I struggled to steady my thoughts, persuading myself that surely this was an unfortunate coincidence, an unrelated event, perhaps a death in the family of the maid.

"I could not bear to stay, and yet I could not bear to leave. I returned to the room, closing the door shut behind me, and tried everything in my power to revive Isabella. She responded to nothing, until just a few minutes before my allotted time was to run out: she gave a long, deep sigh, and moved her head. I could see fleeting eye movement beneath her eyelids. Excited with this development, I spoke to her, asking questions, anything that would require a response, rubbing her hands and her face, knocking on various objects around her to see if she could hear. But alas, nothing. I determined to keep trying. I planned on making a few phone calls that afternoon to colleagues elsewhere in Europe and America. It would all come, as I surely need not tell you, to far too little far too late.

"On that fateful day, my usual two hours with Isabella were extended to nearly three. The master of the house, who usually knocked on the door to announce the driver was waiting downstairs, failed to do so, and I was left to depart on my own. I kept glancing at my watch, mystified as to the delay, but hoping that each passing minute would not be the last. Perhaps, I thought, the master of the house had had time to reflect upon our conversation and decided to grant me more time than usual to tend to Isabella; the only other scenario I could paint for myself was that he was attending to the maid's apparent family matter.

"Neither was, of course, the case," the doctor added.

"That night, as the rain pounded the roof of my hotel, I sat by the fireplace and sifted all of the bits of evidence I had gathered. I went over every detail again and again, piecing them together this way or that... but nothing quite put together a probable hypothesis. I could not assign any significance to the Arab connection, or the Spanish one for that matter, although I supposed, at the time, this to be the least of the mysteries. How little I knew! I desperately wanted to save Isabella, to be free of this nightmarish assignment, to be back in Cordoba practicing my trade and teaching, for those were the things I loved most, but it was—as you know—not to be.

"The next morning was to bring me the fulfillment of the second wish, although accompanied by the cruel laughter of Fate. The driver arrived about 20 minutes late. I remember he was late that day because he had never been late before; but at the time I naturally thought nothing of it. I was only too happy to have another hot tea.

"We arrived at the house just as day broke: for the first time I saw the front garden illuminated with the brilliant rays of the rising sun, dew glittering like long-forgotten jewels on the petals of an impressive collection of roses. It was the last time I ever saw this, or any other garden, as a free man."

The doctor looked off into the distance, into a distant yet tragic past that I, as his listener, could only imagine. I thought, what is a memory good for, in the end, if it must always be only a memory enclosed in the prison of impossibility? I said nothing while he gazed through the window, nothing out of respect for him and nothing because nothing could give him back his life that he lost so unjustly.

"I mounted the long and winding staircase," resumed the doctor, "and entered Isabella's room, as had become my habit the last three weeks. I noted a strange, almost palpable silence throughout the house, but assigned little importance to it. My most fervent desire was to wake Isabella and nurse her back to health.

"But it was not to be, alas! She lay in her bed, brilliant as the sun that bathed her pale cheeks, but when I bent down over her to check her breathing, as I did every morning, I found none to be spared. Alarmed, I checked her pulse. Her blood had ceased to flow and lay rigid in her veins. Death had preceded me—and had already claimed this precious treasure destined, I had been certain, to be mine to save.

"It felt as if a sword of ice had cleft my skull. My hands trembling, my blood churning an icy fire, I gathered Isabella in my arms and gently lifted her. To my horror, her head fell backwards at a strange angle, her throat having been severed and the wound having been cleaned and cleverly hidden by her blanket pulled up close under her chin! Her blood, spilled by the butcher's knife, had seeped into the sheets, an ignominious signature of the awful crime.

"As I held the unfortunate young thing in my arms, my right hand holding her head and neck together, I glanced at the pillow and there saw, scrawled in an unsteady hand, a single phrase in Arabic lettering. I reached out with my left hand and touched the writing—the ink was not yet dry.

"I uttered a cry of agony—for I had been but seconds too late! I cursed the driver who had failed to arrive on time, I cursed forever all the glasses of Moroccan tea the Spanish never drink, I cursed the dewdrops on the petals of roses in beautiful gardens, I cursed my own inability to prevent this death of one so young."

My gut in knots, I desperately wanted to know what the phrase said.

"My mind raged with terror and fury—if you can imagine the intensity of the fire that consumed my being at that moment." The doctor's voice dropped hard and cold, his eyes engulfed in a rage that had not, after these 21 years, dissipated. And yes, I could imagine the terror and fury. I could imagine—and understand.

"Nothing remained for me but to find the assassin— or assassins, whoever and however many they were. Gently I lay Isabella down. I stood up over her, mesmerized by how beautiful she looked even in death... and just then, involuntarily, my hand slid into my coat pocket. There, I felt a piece of paper—I extracted it—it was the fraudulent prescription. I stared at the writing on the pillow, unable to believe my own eyes: the hand was the same! The maid!

"I burst forth from the room and flew down the cursed stairs. I cared neither for the master nor any other inhabitant of the house who would have tried to stop me in my way, for my fury was far greater and driven by far more righteous passions than any they would have ever known; the maid was the object of my deadly desire then, and nothing could have stopped me in my tracks.

"Nothing—except the absence of a single living soul in the entire house. I searched through the home without tiring, until a momentary pause at the bottom of the stairs permitted a single thought to enter my brain: they had gone, the assassins, and I the only suspect at the scene of the crime! But as all events that took place these past few days, this thought, too, had come too late. For just then"—the doctor closed his eyes for a moment—"just then the door opened, forced open by the police chief. Our eyes met, and in his I saw the condemnation of the rest of my life."

The doctor was visibly worn out by the recounting of the story. He closed his eyes and held on to the armrests of his chair for a few moments, his hands trembling. I waited, respectfully, in silence.

Presently he came to, and released his grip on the chair. He reached for his tea.

"Have you no questions, then?" he said simply.

The fact was that my pen had stopped in mid-air some time ago; I had taken practically no notes since that initial burst of energy. I stared at the nearly blank pages, suddenly spent.

"Too many," I said. "But one above all. What did the phrase in Arabic mean?"

The doctor waved his hand in that characteristic way of his. He shook his head meaningfully, his eyes warning me not to insist. This was a secret that he wanted to die with him.

"All I can tell you, my good man, is that it didn't say what you might think it said."

I would have loved to have something to think.

"I imagine you have no more time. I have kept you here surely far longer than your editor would like," the doctor said, lowering his voice confidentially.

"I have a few moments more," I said, picking up on his offered confidence. The doctor had grown to trust me, and I wanted to maintain that trust.

"Very well. I shall finish—it is only fair to you, having come all this way. Before the chief of police led me into the inevitable car waiting outside, I asked for a moment to gather my things upstairs in Isabella's room. Naturally he was not about to let me out of his sight, and certainly not allow me back into the presence of the victim alone, but upon assuring him I would cooperate completely with everything he asked of me, he followed me up the stairs as the rest of his officers began to file into the house. He, too, was visibly moved upon seeing Isabella, but maintained his composure and began conducting the business of processing the crime scene even as he kept a tight eye on me. I was allowed to take only my keys, my wallet, and my coat: my medical bag was, as could be expected, swiftly confiscated.

"None of that mattered. You see, all I really wanted was another chance to look at the writing on the pillow. Earlier, when I laid Isabella back down, I'd moved her onto another pillow, purely out of respect—the ink was fresh, as I mentioned, and I did not want it to soil her hair, even in death. But I had been far too rash in my reaction, and had not taken the time to read the verse. I now had a second chance to imprint the fateful phrase in my head forever."

My pulse raced. "You know what it said, doctor."

"I know enough to tell you that no one I had come into contact with at that house was responsible for Isabella's murder," replied the doctor. "And I know," he added softly, "that had I kept my composure, had I taken a moment to read it the first time, you and I would not be sitting here today."

I knew no living force, benign or otherwise, would persuade the doctor to unburden his heart that had been closed for so long. I tried a different tack, teetering on that fine line between ethics and journalistic objectivity.

"If that is true, surely you have enough evidence to expose the true assassins and regain your freedom."

"Many have suggested the same. It is, however, not for me to expose them. The house was sold shortly thereafter—the family, sick with grief, moved away from Madrid. I found out that the man who had supervised my work and whom I have been referring to as the master of the house, was the family's accountant."

"Why would an accountant be in charge of overseeing the work of a medical doctor?" I said, incredulous. "And where was the family, then, all this time? Was it not someone within the family who you believe committed, or ordered, the murder?"

"Several of the family members had been overseas," said the doctor in reply to my second question, but offering no more information on the point, or my other questions. "I never discovered—until recently—the motives behind for this most bizarre sequence of events."

The doctor looked at me searchingly, as if determining whether he should go on. Something in my expression must have convinced him to continue.

"The accountant, also convicted, died in prison not long ago. Shortly before his incarceration, I received a sealed letter from him—and mind you," smiled the doctor, "the envelope was tightly sealed and stamped with his initials, to ensure me that it had not been tampered with—for you see he had not forgotten the incident of the duplicate prescription—in which he told me everything. He begged my forgiveness, sure that I would not give it, and pledged his soul to save mine. It was the letter of a man condemned not only by law and the fickle winds of politics, but by his own religion and conscience, a man, in his own words, damned for all eternity."

"It *was* him, then...?"

The doctor shook his head meaningfully. "As I said, no one I had met in that house was responsible. In fact, rather the contrary. Rather the contrary."

"Forgive me, doctor, but I fail to follow. If in fact the accountant was not the assassin, if indeed he disclosed 'everything,' as you say, and if indeed you know what the phrase said, then, I dare say, you hold the keys to your own freedom!"

"One innocent man cannot gain his freedom at the expense of another," said the doctor.

"But the accountant is—"

"True, true," the doctor interrupted. "He is no longer here to enjoy the freedom that should have been his. But given who his employers were and the circumstances in which Isabella died, it was a freedom that would have come with a heavy price in any situation."

The doctor waved his hand in his characteristic way. His eyes, brilliant and alive, smiled at me.

"As for mine, it is too late for freedom, my son. I would not know what to do with it."

* * *

It had begun to rain and I, unable to let go of the doctor's voice in my head, looked out the car window through the rivulets twisting along the glass. Passers-by had become smudges of color flitting by, intermittently obscured by passing cars. I stared at my note pad. I already knew the story I was going to write: it certainly wasn't what my editor expected, or, for that matter, what the rest of Madrid could have dreamed of in the wee hours of the morning.

My focus fixed on the address the doctor had given me, I abruptly decided to pay homage to the unjust derailing of a man's life. I asked the driver to drop me off in the Chamartin area; from there I took another taxi to the cursed street. I had no umbrella; the rain fell heavier now. *No matter,* I thought to myself, waving my hand in the doctor's characteristic gesture. I walked down the street, searching for the number 32—and already I could see it: an impressive mass of white stucco and red Spanish tiles, encircled by a thick wall. I stopped in front of the outer gate. Thick, unforgiving wood, a large iron lock and handle, and there, to the left carved into the wall, the mailbox with its now rusty hinge. I took my pen and lifted the cover, the image of the doctor in this same precise spot decades ago burning in my mind.

There, sure enough, was the name, the insidious name, still partially visible in that muted gold lettering beneath the name of the new owners.

A cold shiver titillated down my back. I was seized by an irresistible compulsion to interview the new family, whoever they were. I wasn't a journalist for nothing—the story could be made that much more relevant if I included an interview with the current inhabitants of the house— did they know they were living in a house that had been the scene of a horrific murder and a terrible injustice hidden for over twenty years?

I rang the bell.

Perhaps no one was home. I would come back another day, and another day, and another until someone was. But

Providence was with me. A female voice answered through the intercom: *¿Quién es?*

I explained who I was and that I was here for an interview about an important story that took place in this house, for a top newspaper in Madrid. The voice told me to wait and hung up. I waited. Within moments a key was inserted into the gate from the other side, turned in the ancient mechanism of the lock, and the door slowly creaked open to reveal a diminutive older lady who bore, nonetheless, the air of a noblewoman.

Scanning me up and down with a cautious, experienced air, she determined within a few seconds I really was who I said I was, and ushered me into the courtyard. The front door of the house, a heavy weather-stained wooden door, swelled imposing and impenetrable to me but slid immediately open with her touch.

Inside was warm and inviting, a fire crackling in the sitting room, an antique clock softly ticking a relaxed monologue. The lady of the house bid me to make myself at home. I must be frozen solid, walking around in that rain without an umbrella. She must be sure to give me one before I leave.

Not the cold impersonal household the doctor had described. How things change.

My hostess called for her housekeeper, ordering hot coffee and a bit of cake. As I settled in on a settee near the fireplace, my hostess opposite me on a decidedly luxurious sofa, the housekeeper brought in a silver tray with two steaming cups of rich coffee and the requisite slices of cake.

The coffee struck me as strange—I had expected tea.

I looked up to thank the housekeeper; she had a dark olive complexion, features I would have described as Middle Eastern, jet-black hair tinged with a spice of gray. I guessed she was in her sixties, although with none of the usual attendant fatigue for that age. She nodded briefly in acknowledgment.

I got my interview, although it was rather short. My hostess, whose husband she said was away overseas on business, did not know much about Dr. --- or the murder, but she was properly saddened to hear about it and certainly hoped that the poor girl's soul rest in peace after all her suffering. No doubt the dear woman's somewhat indifferent reaction had much to do with her being successfully removed from the pains and struggles of the lives of others; even if those others were just as wealthy as she, or perhaps more so. It was not my place to judge.

I inquired politely if I might possibly take a peek at the room. At this, my amiable hostess suddenly bristled, pressing her gaze fiercely into me. She failed to see why that would be necessary; this was her home, not a haunted museum. I put my pen and notepad respectfully down in front of her, assuring her I had neither camera nor tape recorder, and would take no notes by hand. I simply wanted to pay my personal respects to this story that had gripped all of Spain 21 years ago.

The hostess reflected on my request a few moments, swaying in her thoughts from one answer to the other, but in the end she rose to show me the way. I followed, not daring tell her that I already knew it. I climbed the long winding staircase behind her, my hands running along the polished wooden railing that had felt the touch of the good doctor and kept his secret all these years.

At the top of the staircase, she opened the door—still painted white—for me and stepped aside. She advised me she would be downstairs and that I could take my time. *Gracias, señora,* I said.

The room, to my considerable surprise, was exactly as the doctor described it. The bed with the white linen, the chair he had spent so many hours on, the small writing desk. My stomach tightened. It could not be. Twenty-one years! On impulse, I walked to the window. Outside I could see a lush garden of roses stretching for nearly a city block, the stone wall visible through the rose bushes.

The sky was a strange shade of milky gray; it had stopped raining. I shivered. Thoughts, connections, hypotheses raged in my head, each less rational than the previous.

A bit breathless, I reached for the latch to open the window, but it would not immediately give... *as if it had been recently painted.* I pressed harder, and the latch made a sharp crack—

I heard a soft gasp behind me. My heart stung cold. I turned around, half expecting to see Isabella there in bed, deep asleep. It was the housekeeper, bearing a silver tray with what looked like a cold compress. She had apparently not expected anyone to be here, for she stood frozen for a few moments in the middle of the room, looking at me, I looking at her.

In that strange, silent span of time, I felt something hauntingly familiar about her.

She was the first to break the impasse: she came closer and extended the tray toward me, gesturing that I should take the compress. I had been imagining things: it was not a cold compress but a hot towelette to wash my hands. It occurred to me only much later that there was no logic in her bringing me a hot towel; but at that moment I accepted it without hesitation and pressed it to my forehead. The heat of the towel brought me halfway back to my senses. I replaced the towel on the tray.

"Shokran," I said, surprising myself.

The woman's eyes flashed with momentary panic, which she quickly suppressed.

"La shokra ala wajib," she muttered, and left the room.

I stood as if nailed to the floor. *It cannot be,* I feverishly repeated to myself. I refused to believe she was the maid, Isabella's maid, and yet nothing, but nothing could convince me otherwise. Her features, her age, her language, and the room.... My cold-headed journalist's mind dug in obstinate, yet I had no choice but to accept the facts as they were, whether they made sense or not. It was not my place to rearrange reality.

I stood there in the middle of the room for some time, alone and in silence, staring at the empty white bed, the doctor's story pounding through my brain.

I finally pulled in the will to leave, but on my way out I paused by the bed, imagining myself as the doctor leaning over an unconscious Isabella. There, on the pillow, an unsteady hand had scrawled a verse in Arabic. I reached out my hand on impulse—the ink was not yet dry.

STORY SEED

*Every story I write contains a seed of origin,
a kernel of real life that inspires the story.
This is the seed of "Verse in Arabic."*

In the fall of 1998, I was living in Madrid, enrolled in a professional international relations program at the Instituto Universitario Ortega y Gasset. To supplement my financial resources, I taught English on the side, mostly to Spanish firms or the Spanish branches of U.S. companies. One of my classes was the Madrid office of the Boston Consulting Group.

One morning, one of my students came rushing through the door several minutes before class began. He sat into his chair with peculiar determination.

"¿Algo pasó?" I said. "Something wrong?"

My student hesitated, a quick glance to confirm there was no one else in class, then lowered his voice and leaned in a little.

"I had to fire my maid," he said, in Spanish. I raised an eyebrow. "Yes, yes, I had to fire her because she wrote something on my pillow."

"She wrote on your pillow." I had to repeat it to make sure I heard right.

He nodded vehemently.

"I came back from a business trip and found this strange writing on my pillow. It can only be her, she's the only one with access to my apartment."

"What did it say?"

"I don't know, she wrote it in Arabic. I don't read Arabic and she speaks little Spanish."

My writer's soul fired up, conjuring dramatic scenes of clandestine activities, high-level political intrigue, links this "maid" had in the Middle East and possibly elsewhere. Critical, I thought, absolutely critical to find out what the writing says.

"You should probably find out what the writing says," I suggested as nonchalantly as I could. "Or if you like, bring it into class and we'll find a translator."

My student nodded, still visibly disturbed but nowhere near as interested as I was in the mysterious writing.

I spent the entire week unable to stop thinking about this bizarre event, running scenarios in my mind that would explain the writing on my student's pillow. Each more fantastic than the previous, none made any plausible sense. I had literally nothing to go on.

When the next day of class finally arrived the following week, I waited impatiently for him to walk through the door. Once again he arrived a little ahead of time, perhaps the only Spaniard in all of Spain to be so punctual. He said *good morning*, I said *good morning*; we exchanged the usual pleasantries. Unable to contain my curiosity any longer, I asked him about the writing on the pillow.

"So... that pillow your maid wrote on... did you get the writing translated?"

"No," he replied. "I had the pillow washed. I don't really care what it said, I just don't want it in my house."

And so, as simple as that, the message of the mysterious Arabic writing on the pillow disappeared forever. The bottom dropped out from my stomach. The loss was irrevocable, but profoundly significant. Without it, this story would never come to be.

I taught another English class, a group of young Spanish attorneys, on Tuesday and Thursday mornings. I always walked to that class as it was relatively close to my apartment, and I loved having time to think, which you don't tend to have if you're in the subway, on the bus, or in a taxi. At least not in Spain.

And so, for the next several weeks, I spent those early morning walks down the long Calle --- immersed in the mystery of these words, this phrase, this verse written in Arabic on my student's pillow. It was fall, and the cool, foggy mornings, warmed by hot chocolate and croissants served in nameless cafés, invigorated my imagination. But a writer who truly respects her craft keeps her ego out of it. Stories are sacred, and must be allowed to tell themselves. So I walked and I listened. Intently. I listened and I let the strange story of the words written in Arabic work itself out, on its own terms.

What materialized during those brisk morning walks surprised even me: a chilling tale of wrongful imprisonment involving a renowned medical doctor, an innocent young girl, an absentee yet apparently loving family, and a household of strangers whose actions and motives alike escaped all logic. And a punch line like no other I had written before: "the ink was not yet dry." That, I instantly knew, was *la phrase clé, el intríngulis,* the arrow through the heart of the plotline. Ironically, I had the punch line but not the context. I had no idea what the verse in Arabic meant or who wrote it, and therefore could not finish the story.

What I mean by "finish" has nothing to do with the typical temporal construct of linear time, as in coming to the end of something. The end of the story was already on paper. What was missing was the DNA of the mystery, that little twist in the plot that would give the punch line its full, most potent impact.

It wasn't until fourteen years later that it would finally come to me. I had put the manuscript away, filed in a digital folder on my desktop for years while I built my company and plotted our escape with my husband from the searing cold of the Northeast. The warm California sun thawed all those stories that lay frozen in time, but it was especially this one that ripened a much richer fruit.

How did it happen? I listened. Again. But this time I listened longer, closer, deeper. I had gotten to know the characters subsconsciously, over those fourteen years, and they were now sharing much more of their story with me, a story that demagnetizes our own contemporary moral compass.

It's time for me to share it with you.

DIALOGUE

A story should never end the conversation it starts. In fact, literature should serve as a looking glass for our times and for our minds, as it always has for generations and cultures past. It should be a cup of fresh-brewed coffee, a relaxing but oh-so-potent drink at the end of a long day.

This is why I devote a series of blogs on my author's site to my stories—in this case, a blog to discuss freedom, medical ethics, and personal integrity and honor that "Verse in Arabic" invites us to explore:

www.birgitterasine.com/blog/freedom

Check out the blog and join the conversation!

CONNECT WITH BIRGITTE

Birgitte is a socially connected author. Reach out!

Web

www.birgitterasine.com

Facebook

www.facebook.com/birgitterasine

Twitter

twitter.com/birgitte_rasine

Pinterest

pinterest.com/birgitterasine

Google Plus

http://bit.ly/Z8M1ef

ABOUT THE AUTHOR

Czech-American author Birgitte Rasine writes literary fiction that pulls the beauty and the pain of the human experience out into the open by their very roots. It's raw, it's romantic, and it's real. Every story Birgitte writes is born from an actual event or experience, and probes the deeper, if inconvenient, truths about our psyche and modern society.

In her professional lifetime, Birgitte has sported a great many writer's hats: journalist, poet, playwright, screenwriter, business editor, copywriter. She composed her first poem at the age of six in Czech, her native language, reciting it in the evenings to her baby sister when they were both supposed to be sleeping. A few years later, the family emigrated to the United States to flee from political persecution and to give the girls a better education in the West. Birgitte's love of storytelling would take her through film studies at Stanford University to the world of Hollywood, to living abroad and working on social and environmental issues.

During those years, she traveled and she talked to people. Everywhere. Climate scientists, academicians, waiters, students, government officials, taxi drivers, business people, artists, attorneys, and activists—in airports and train stations, in cafés and restaurants, conferences and business meetings, on film sets and on the street.

It was the travels and the face-to-face conversations that enriched Birgitte's innate curiosity about human society and fed the fires of her propensity to probe beyond the usual pleasantries of social relationships and ask the tougher, deeper questions. These fleeting but powerful experiences have, like grapes slowly maturing on the vine, shaped Birgitte's signature literary style, the "stream of consciousness" stories that debuted with "Confession."

In addition to her writing, Birgitte serves as the Chief Evolution Officer (CEO) of LUCITÀ Inc., a hybrid design and communications firm based in Silicon Valley. She is a member of several professional organizations, including the Association of Women in Water, Energy and Environment, and sits on the board of directors of the American Fund for Czech and Slovak Leadership Studies in New York City. She is descended from the late Dr. Alois Rašín, co-founder of Czechoslovakia (1918) and the nation's first Minister of Finance.

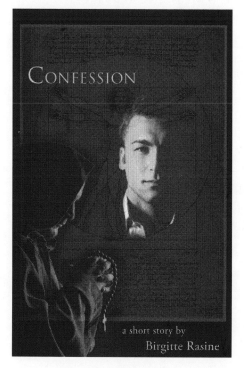

BAKALY
a short story

Traveling in the Russian countryside on a trip home after many years abroad, a young expatriot finds himself lost one night in a small town. He stumbles into an underground casino, and his life changes forever—overnight. But it's not the kind of "golden jackpot" story you might expect... or ever hope for yourself.

Available in print or as an eBook for most major eReaders including the iPad, Nook, and Kindle/Kindle Fire.

THE SERPENT AND THE JAGUAR
non fiction

Discover the Tzolk'in, the sacred calendar the Maya have used for millennia to guide their personal and spiritual lives, and why it's more relevant than ever to our modern lifestyle. Learn how to integrate the concept of sacred time that this calendar keeps into your busy life. Includes daily energy texts for each day of the Tzolk'in cycle, Mayan calendar tables, and descriptions of the 20 day signs and the 13 numbers.

Available in print or as an eBook for most major eReaders including the iPad, Nook, and Kindle/Kindle Fire.

Thoughts & Reflections

Thoughts & Reflections

Thoughts & Reflections

Made in the USA
Charleston, SC
14 July 2013